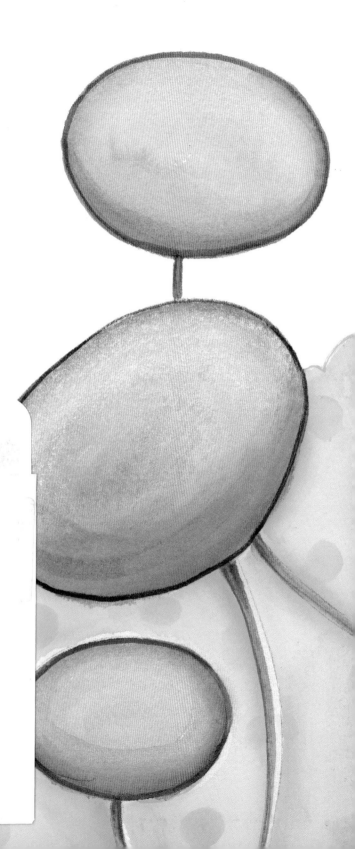

Dance with Me

To Mum and Dad, for music, books and memories. – PH

For Kyle, who can and will dance. – GJ

First published 2016

EK Books
an imprint of Exisle Publishing Pty Ltd
'Moonrising', Narone Creek Road, Wollombi, NSW 2325, Australia
P.O. Box 60–490, Titirangi, Auckland 0642, New Zealand
www.ekbooks.org

A CiP record for this book is available from the National Library of Australia.

ISBN 978-1-925335-23-1

Designed by Big Cat Design
Typeset in Warnock Pro 20/33pt
Printed in China

This book uses paper sourced under ISO 14001 guidelines from well-managed
forests and other controlled sources.

10 9 8 7 6 5 4 3 2 1

Dance with Me

Penny Harrison

Illustrated by Gwynneth Jones

There was once a ballerina who lived in a small, wooden box.
The ballerina stood straight and tall in her ribboned dance shoes and looked out over a field of flowers and beyond to the turquoise sea.

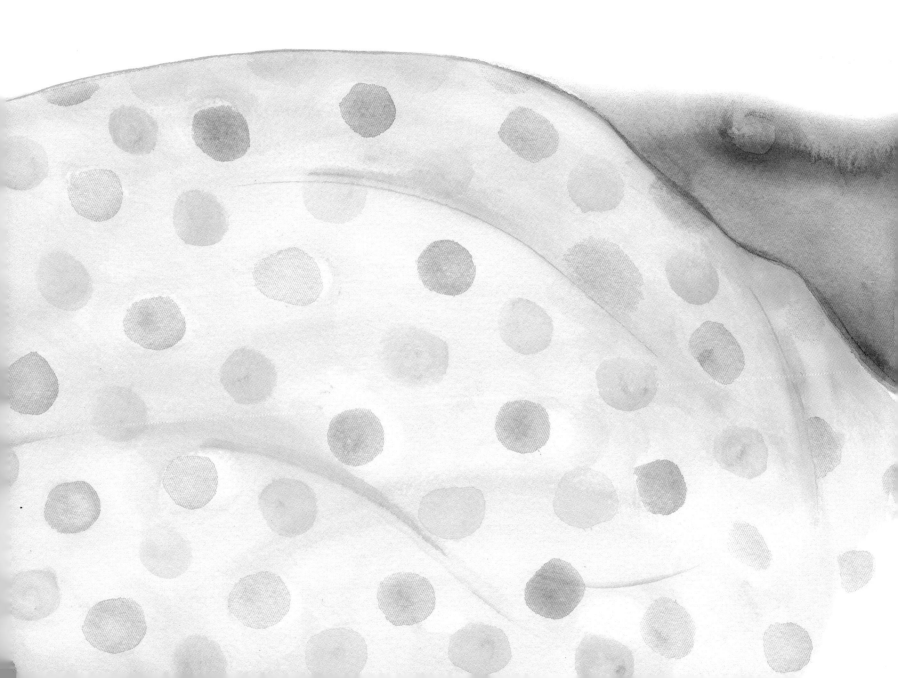

Each day, a little girl appeared before her and the ballerina twirled and whirled and swayed and swirled and sang to the little girl, 'Come, dance with me.'

And the little girl would
laugh and clap her hands and
dance with the ballerina.

But the years passed and the little girl grew, as little girls do,
and soon she did not have time to dance with the ballerina.

So, one day, the ballerina jumped down from her wooden box. She skipped across the windowsill and leapt into the field of flowers, where she waltzed around the roses and flitted through freesias, until she came to a bee.

And the ballerina twirled and whirled and swayed and
swirled and sang to the bee, 'Come, dance with me.'

But the busy bee buzzed, 'Too much to do, little ballerina.
No time to dance.'

So the ballerina danced away, down to the edge of the ocean. And she frolicked in the shallows and skipped in the sand, until she spotted a turtle.

And the ballerina twirled and whirled and swayed and swirled and sang to the turtle, 'Come, dance with me.'

But the turtle muttered grumpily, 'Turtles don't dance, you silly ballerina.' And it shuffled into the sea.

The ballerina hopped across the rocks and bounded onto a boat.

She set sail for an island where she spun through the vines, until she spied a leopard.

And the ballerina twirled and whirled and
swayed and swirled and sang to the leopard,
'Come, dance with me.'

But the leopard bared its teeth and snarled,
'I'd rather eat you for dinner, little ballerina!'

The ballerina hopped and skipped and
jumped away, and returned to her box,
just as the girl came into the room.

And the ballerina twirled and whirled and
swayed and swirled and sang to the girl,
'Come, dance with me.'

But the girl closed the lid.

The music stopped. The ballerina was still.

The box was packed away for many years.

Until one day …

The lid was opened and the ballerina, sleepy
and bent, slowly moved, until she stood straight
and tall in her ribboned dance shoes ...

and looked out over a green forest and a tranquil lake ...

... into the face of a little girl, just like
the one she used to know.

And the little girl twirled and whirled and swayed and
swirled and sang to the ballerina, 'Come, dance with me.'

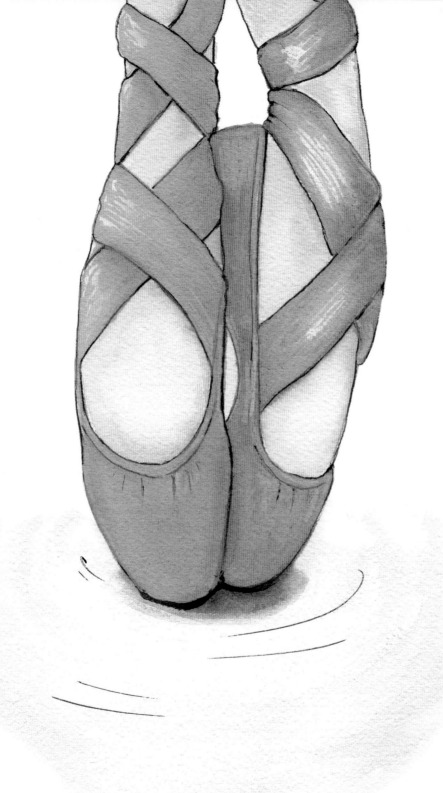